The Boat in the Tree

This book is for Gabe—*T.W.J.*

To my mum and dad—*J.S.*

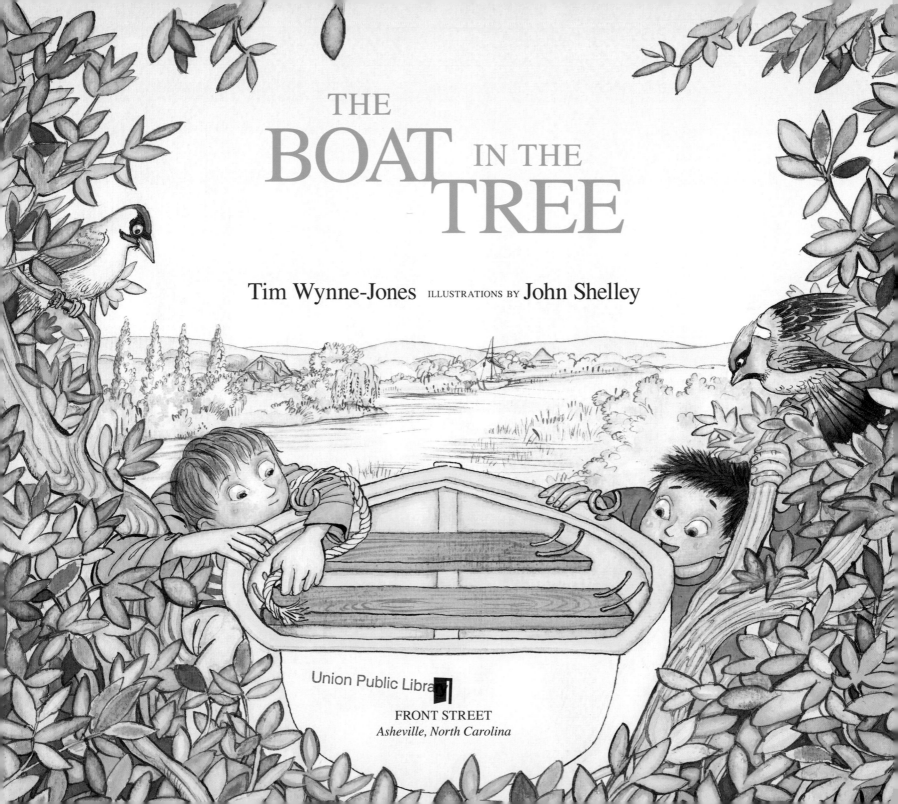

THE BOAT IN THE TREE

Tim Wynne-Jones   ILLUSTRATIONS BY John Shelley

FRONT STREET
Asheville, North Carolina

Library of Congress Cataloging-in-Publication Data

Wynne-Jones, Tim.
The boat in the tree / by Tim Wynne-Jones ; illustrations by John Shelley.
p. cm.
Summary: Having dreamed of sailing to Bongadongo since the day his
younger brother was adopted, a boy finally has his means of escape
but cannot make use of it without his brother's help.
ISBN-13: 978-1-932425-49-9 (hardcover : alk. paper)
[1. Boats and boating—Fiction. 2. Brothers—Fiction. 3. Adoption—Fiction.
4. Sibling rivalry—Fiction.] I. Shelley, John, ill. II. Title.
PZ7.W993Bnw 2007
[Fic]—dc22
2006011722

FRONT STREET
An Imprint of Boyds Mills Press, Inc.
A Highlights Company

815 Church Street
Honesdale, Pennsylvania 18431

The day Mom and Dad went to pick up my new brother, I built a raft.

I borrowed Dad's hammer and nails without asking.
I used a lot of nails and a lot of wood and an old door and
a sheet and a broomstick and set sail for Bongadongo.

Mom and Dad came home with Simón.
"Watch out for the sharks," I warned him.

On my birthday, Grandfather gave me a ship in a bottle.

"How do they do it?" I asked.

"With strings," he said.

I looked at my ship all the time.
Very close.
Too close.

"Hold fast!" I cried.
"Reel in the anchor,
roll out the mainsails.
Next stop, Bongadongo!"

I saved up my allowance to buy a boat
—the *Bounty*. I did all the gluing myself.
And the painting, too.

Then I saved up my allowance and
bought another boat—the *Bismarck*.
I built a whole fleet.

I hung my fleet from the ceiling. And I went to sleep dreaming of faraway places.

One day late that spring, I found a real boat.

You couldn't read the name anymore, and weeds were growing through the bottom.
I borrowed Dad's hammer and nails. And his saw, too. I asked first.

I fixed the holes. But it still leaked.
So I saved up my allowance and bought some gum.
A *lot* of gum.

It worked.
Sort of.

"I need a boat. A real boat."

"One day," said Mom.

"That will take a lot of allowance," said Dad.

"In time," said Grandfather.

"I want out of here," I said.
"What's the problem?" said Mom.
"Him!" I shouted.

Nobody listened to me.
Nobody cared.
So I ran away.

Down by the river, the wind was starting to blow. But I wasn't going home.

"I can tie a reef knot and read a map, and I'm not afraid

of scurvy or sharks or … typhoooooooooons!"

When the sun came out again, I heard Simón calling me.
"Come on," he said. "You've got to see this."

There was a boat. A real boat. A new boat.
It was up in a tree.
"If only we could get it down," said Simón.

"We'll need rope," I said.
"I'll get some," said Simón.

We had to pull very hard.

We pulled and pulled and didn't give up.

It was a bit banged up, but there were no holes. It was light.
We carried that boat right down to the shore all by ourselves.